Food Freak

Alex Van Tol

orca currents

ORCA BOOK PUBLISHERS

Library and Archives Canada Cataloguing in Publication

Van Tol, Alex, author
Food freak / Alex Van Tol.
(Orca currents)

Issued in print and electronic formats.
ISBN 978-1-4598-1339-7 (paperback).—ISBN 978-1-4598-1340-3 (pdf).—
ISBN 978-1-4598-1341-0 (epub)

I. Title. II. Series: Orca currents
PS8643.A63F66 2017   jc813'.6   c2016-904455-6
                            c2016-904456-4

First published in the United States, 2017
Library of Congress Control Number: 2016950084

Summary: In this high-interest novel for middle readers, Dani is mortified by her
father's public rants about the dangers of processed foods.

MIX
Paper from
responsible sources
FSC® C016245

*Orca Book Publishers is dedicated to preserving the environment and has
printed this book on Forest Stewardship Council® certified paper.*

Orca Book Publishers gratefully acknowledges the support for its
publishing programs provided by the following agencies: the Government
of Canada through the Canada Book Fund and the Canada Council
for the Arts,and the Province of British Columbia through
the BC Arts Council and the Book Publishing Tax Credit.

Cover photography by iStock.com
Author photo by BK Studios

ORCA BOOK PUBLISHERS
www.orcabook.com

Printed and bound in Canada.

20 · 19 · 18 · 17 • 4 3 2 1

For Apocalypse Guy

Chapter One

You're never closer to death than at the grocery store. That's what my dad always says.

The way he talks, you would think the Grim Reaper lurks behind every box of cereal and jar of spaghetti sauce, ready to lop off people's heads with his scythe. Sugar. Palm oil. MSG. Preservatives. Saturated fats.

I turn the box of crackers around in my hand and scan the ingredient deck. *Partially hydrogenated vegetable oil.* Nope. As I put the box back on the shelf, I hear Papa's voice in my head: *That stuff clogs your arteries and leads to obesity*.

Maybe I'll have to start making my own crackers. I've already started making our granola bars and yogurt. And we're practically down to only oatmeal for cereal.

I check the brown rice carefully. Looks okay. There's just the one word on the bag: *rice*. I know the avocado and tomatoes will be fine, because they're organic. I don't know about these tortilla chips though. They've only got a few ingredients, which is always a good sign. But on the other hand, I'm not sure about *canola or sunflower oil*. I put them back on the shelf. I'll look it up later.

I walk right past the salad dressings and barbecue sauces. *Jam-packed with sodium benzoate*, Papa would say. *Enhances the flavor of acidic foods. Brilliant for the food industry. Absolutely brilliant. But it causes cancer.*

I don't even go down the soup aisle.

I buy frec-run eggs, not because Papa thinks regular eggs are bad but because I feel sorry for any animal that has to live in a cage that's too small to stand up in.

When I've got everything I need, I pick Maria's lane. There are shorter lines, but I don't care. Maria is the nicest cashier. "How is grade nine going, Dani lovely?" she asks once I reach her till. Her square brown hands move quickly as she passes things over the scanner. The computer beeps as it registers each item. Basil, onions, parmesan cheese, almond flour.

"Grade eight," I say.

"Ah, *sí*. You seem so much older," Maria says. "Such a tall and lovely girl is my Dani. You have not been in for long time," she says. "Is nice to be back at school with all your friends?"

I force a smile. "Sure is." She finishes the packing and hands me the receipt. I take it and tuck it into my wallet, then give Maria a nod. "See you soon."

"Sí, Dani, see you soon." And she turns her beaming smile on the next customer.

I head for the exit, a cloth bag in each hand. At the doors, I take a quick look around. I don't want to run into anybody I know.

The coast looks clear. I head outside, dreading what's next. But maybe I'll get off easy today. Maybe the neighborhood weirdo won't be there.

No such luck. He's there, all right, the tall guy with the salt-and-pepper beard

4

and wild gray hair. It's cold out, so today his hair sticks out from under a knit cap. Long face. Lots of wrinkles.

He's dressed nicely enough in black loafers, gray dress pants, tie and button-down shirt. You'd never know he was a freak except that he's wearing a crazycakes sandwich board and holding an even bigger sign on a long stick. All the signs have thick black lettering on them.

He turns slowly, revolving back and forth in a semicircular arc, as usual. He wants to make sure everyone has a chance to read the message on the sandwich board. He waves the long sign back and forth high above him as people hurry toward the store's automatic doors. They all avoid his eyes.

Every time I see him I expect to catch him looking up at the sky and muttering or shaking his fist. So far it hasn't happened. He just stands and turns, watching people as they leave the store with their bags full of death.

Yeah, that's our resident freakomatic.

And, oh so lucky for me, he's also my dad.

Chapter Two

I duck behind a chubby guy and hurry along in his blind spot so that Papa can't see me. If he does, he'll greet me with a "Hallo, Dani! How was your day?" in his thick German accent. Like he's a normal father or something.

It drives me crazy when he talks to me in public, especially when other people are around. One time last spring I was coming out of the store with Joss Jameson, the worst possible person for me to have been with right then. When she saw Papa standing on the boulevard in the parking lot, she curled her lip and said, *God, isn't it* embarrassing *for you that your dad does that all day long?*

Of course it's embarrassing. It kills me with shame. But do you think I was about to let Joss know it?

He doesn't do it all *day long*, I said. *He still works at the university.*

Does he lecture his students about processed foods there too? I could hear the sneer in her voice.

No. Just history. I said it with as much acid as I could muster.

Joss gave a delicate shudder. Then her phone pinged, and she grabbed for it. Thank God.

Now I do my shopping alone.

I've told Papa in a dozen different ways that it's not cool for him to stand around wearing signs about doom and destruction. Especially outside our own grocery store. But he doesn't even hear what I'm saying. *People need to know, Dani*, he always says.

I haven't brought it up with him lately. Now I just do my shopping at Grant's, which is within walking distance from Central Middle School. I don't come to Origins Market very often anymore.

The number 28 bus wheezes to a stop in front of me. Yellow leaves swirl into the doorway as I heave my bags up the stairs. I find a seat near the back and arrange the bags at my feet, then take out my book for the ride home. I open it to the page with my bookmark, but my eyes drift back toward the market entrance. The woman sitting beside me is looking at Papa too. He's still turning this way and that, spreading his message of ruin to all who pass by. She squints a little, and I can see her lips moving slightly as she reads his sign. Then she blinks and faces forward again. I wonder what she's thinking.

Papa is always careful not to stand in any one location for too long. Store owners don't like that. Some days I see him at the market. Other days he's on the corner at the intersection. Sometimes he goes to other parts of the city. But most of the time he stays close to home. Sometimes he stands outside the plaza liquor store or the pharmacy. And the pizza place. That's always great— lots of my old friends go there.

Old friends as in, they aren't my friends anymore. At first they didn't make a big deal of my dad's weirdness. But when it became evident his sign waving wasn't just a phase, when you could see he was in this for the long haul, some people started making fun. Just little jokes here and there, but they hurt.

My social capital at school tanked. Eventually it felt like I was being shunned. So I shunned them back. Why should I try to get along with jerks?

The final straw was when Jordan Rigby showed up at the spring masquerade ball dressed as the Food Freak. He had the sandwich board and the sign and the beard—the whole nine yards. *PROCESSED FOODS = WEAPONS OF MASS DESTRUCTION,* the front of his sandwich board said. In smaller letters below: *INSULIN RESIS-TANCE. HIGH TRIGLYCERIDES. INCREASED FAT + CHOLESTEROL. CANCER.*

There was another sign on his back. *SUGAR IS A KILLER. BASTARDIZA-TION OF THE EARTH'S BOUNTY.* He also had the long pole with another sign at the top. He waved it back and forth, just like Papa does. *JESUS DIED FOR YOUR SINS—BUT YOU'RE DYING*

FOR YOUR FOOD. EXCESS SALT. TRANS FATS.

They were exactly like my dad's signs.

I knew the jig was up when Peyton—my so-called best friend—laughed her guts out. Papa and I had a big fight about it that night. I burst into tears as soon as I got home.

Dani? he asked. *What happened? Did somebody hurt you at the dance?* He was instantly beside me, holding my elbow and patting my hair. I threw him off like he was something disgusting.

Nobody hurt me, I snarled. I could see he was surprised, because he took a step back.

Then what happened? Why are you crying? he asked. He was so confused that I'd almost felt bad for him.

I almost never cry. But oh man, I was crying that night. *Everyone was making fun of you*, I sobbed. Which was an

12

exaggeration. But I wanted him to get it, you know? I wanted him to get what this was *doing* to me. *Jordan Rigby dressed up like you for the masquerade, Papa.*

Jordan? Why does this boy dress like me? Papa asked.

I glared at him through my tears. Was he really that stupid? *Because you wear those*, I said, pointing to the stack of signboards leaning against the wall. *Nobody else's dad stands around wearing a bunch of weird signs.*

Papa didn't like that. His brow got all thunderous then, and he stood up taller. *People need to understand, Dani*, he began. *The food they buy is making them sick!*

But can't you tell people in a different way, Papa? I said. Okay, let's be honest—I was shouting by that time.

Papa got quiet then, and I wondered if I had hurt his feelings. Turns out he was just obsessing about food, as usual.

People are dying left and center, Dani, he said. He always got those sayings wrong. Usually it made me laugh, but I wasn't laughing that night. His blue eyes were wide and earnest, and his hands danced around as he talked. *The food industry is packing our food full of toxic chemicals to make it taste good and selling it cheap. And people say, "Hey, this is cheap, and it tastes so good! I will buy more and eat more!"* He spread his arms wide. *Everybody is being tricked! Everybody is eating fake food! Everybody is getting sick!* His voice started to tremble. *Do you want more people to get sick, Dani? Do you want more people to get sick? Like that?*

He didn't even have to say *like that*. I knew.

All the fight went out of me then. *Of course I don't*, I said. And even though he was being stupid and he was being embarrassing and he was ruining my social life, he was still my Papa. I didn't want to see him cry.

I had seen enough of that.

Chapter Three

After remembering that hopeless conversation with Papa, I don't feel like reading. I'd rather sit and sulk. I close my book again. The bus drones away from the curb.

I sulk my way through the next eleven stops, then hunch homeward through a stiff fall breeze. When I get home I discover that the wind has knocked over one of the big plant pots at the bottom of the stairs. I straighten it, feeling depressed at how dirty and sloppy everything looks. The lawn is way overgrown. It's gone all brown, so it looks even more depressing. I go around back and pick some rosemary and oregano from the garden, which is a tangle of green and brown. I should really get out here and tidy up. But I can never find time to work on the yard.

I open the front door, my hands full of herbs, and look around. The house is a mess too. Mornings are always a rush now. I still haven't got the hang of getting up half an hour earlier so I can bus it all the way across the city to Central.

I kick off my shoes and take my herbs into the kitchen. I put the cereal away and close up the bread bag. At the sound of crinkling plastic, Kevin comes running. He rubs against my legs, almost tripping me as I go to rinse my cereal bowl in the sink. His own bowl is empty.

"Oh, Kev," I say. "I'm sorry. I forgot to feed you this morning." He meows as I pull down a tin of food. I mix it with some kibbles in his bowl.

Mamma's face smiles at me from the photo on the windowsill. In the picture she's standing with Auntie Carlotta in front of their house in Tuscany. Her round face is framed by curls.

That was before she got sick and lost all her hair.

"Mamma, can you please stop Papa from acting crazy?" I ask her, setting Kevin's food on the floor. He dives for it. "I know he only wants to help. But he's so bananas about this. I'm worried that people at Central will find out he's my dad. He already wrecked things for me at Spruce Cliff."

Mamma doesn't reply.

Doesn't matter. I know she can hear me.

"So far, it's going okay," I say, washing my hands. I keep talking as I chop tomatoes, onions and cilantro for fresh salsa. "Two months into the school year, and I'm still invisible. I don't talk to anyone, and nobody really pays me any attention. But if anybody ever finds out the wacko sign guy is my dad, I'll have to change schools again. I don't want to change schools again, Mamma."

Rinse, shake, chop, scrape.

I nod, carrying on our imaginary conversation. "Yeah, maybe you're right. Homeschooling might be the way to go." There's something about preparing food that makes it easier to talk about important stuff. My favorite with Mamma was making pies. They were so detailed that she and I could have a good long talk while we rubbed the butter into the flour, rolled out the pastry, and peeled and chopped the apples. We did a lot of kitchen talking, Mamma and I. Pie talking. Bread talking. Ravioli talking.

"I don't mind the idea of doing school at home," I continue. "I think I'm smart enough to keep up. Except I couldn't handle being inside this house all day. Not in the state it's in now." I look over into the living room. God, this place needs a vacuuming. The corners are decorated with drifts of cat hair, silverfish skeletons and dead spiders.

It would be nice if Papa helped out. But he doesn't have the time. Whenever he isn't teaching, he's out preaching. Our living room has been taken over by poster board and plywood and paint. A hammer teeters on the edge of the piano bench. An old coffee can bristles with paintbrushes. It's his workshop. He's like a demented Santa who exclusively makes signs that proclaim the end of humankind and then goes out into the world, bearing gifts for everyone in ALL CAPS.

Papa is convinced that processed foods killed my mother. It was the meats, he says. All the prosciutto and capocollo and salami and pepperoni and mortadella. Mamma's cancer came from the nitrates. Papa is certain that's what did it, even though Mamma usually bought her meats from the Italian deli and not from the supermarket, where they sell the stuff that's mass-produced and full of chemicals.

I think he needed something to blame.

I finish grating the cheese for the (organic, free-range) chicken enchiladas. I leave the salsa to sit, then head for the laundry room. I pile clothes into the washer. I have to be careful not to fill the machine more than halfway, or it'll leak all over the floor. Twice now I've reminded Papa to get it fixed.

At the bottom of the basket is a pair of Papa's pants. As I stuff them into the washer, I notice some weird crusty stuff splattered on one of the pant legs. There are all these little bits of white stuff stuck to it. I pick one off and examine it. It's eggshell.

Somebody threw eggs at my dad.

Rage surges inside me, and I feel my mouth go tight. How dare anybody throw eggs at my father?

Because he's a freakazoid wack-job, that's why.

But it kills me that someone would throw eggs at him. Do you throw eggs at a kid with autism? At a little old man who takes forever to cross the street? At the people who dance around with signs advertising the pizza specials?

I guess some people do. I try not to think about the expression he might have had on his face when he realized someone had egged him. How hurt he must have felt.

One by one, I begin to pick off the shells. What's next? Paint bombs? My anger slowly turns to frustration and then to shame. Why can't Papa just be normal and do normal things? If this processed-food issue is so important to him, why can't he just write articles about it like a regular professor? Why does he have to stand on the street corner and make a fool of himself in public?

Why does he have to make a fool of me?

Chapter Four

I'm always hungry by the time the bell rings for lunch. I packed a chicken gyro today.

As I arrange the onions and tomatoes around the roasted chicken, my thoughts are already on what I'll make for supper. Maybe I'll play around with sweet-potato chips tonight. Thinly sliced sweet potatoes, oiled and salted and then baked until they're crispy. A little rosemary? Or no—a touch of ancho chili pepper. And a squeeze of lime. My mouth waters at the thought.

"That looks amazing."

I look up as Erykah, a slim girl with dancing black eyes, lowers herself into the seat across from me. I've noticed she's friendly to everyone. But I don't want company right now. Or ever.

"I wish *I* had such a nice lunch," she continues. She slings her bag onto the table and opens it up, theatrically unpacking everything to show me how lame her lunch is. I watch as she lines up a container of Jell-O, a baggie of whole-wheat crackers and two little wax-wrapped rounds of cheese.

"You have Babybel—what are you talking about? That stuff is awesome," says Shanna. She sits down beside Erykah and sneaks one of the cheeses. Erykah nods her permission.

Shanna unpacks her lunch: a salami sandwich, a mandarin and an apple juice.

I could tell her that salami will give her cancer, but I don't. "Thanks," I say to Erykah. "It's just a chicken gyro." I knew I should have stuck to eating my lunch by my locker. This is what happens when I decide to eat at the center court like a regular person. I should just get up and walk away. I sit there, weighing the value of staying invisible against the risk of having these two girls see me as totally rude.

I decide to stay but be my most boring self. Maybe they'll realize I suck and go away.

"Chicken gyro," Erykah repeats, eyeing my pita. "It looks like it walked right out of the pages of a fancy food magazine."

Shanna raises her eyebrows. "Since when do you read food magazines?"

She punches the little straw through the hole in her juice box. I consider telling her about the study that found lead in juice boxes.

Erykah shrugs. "My mom does. They're all over the house. She's always trying some new thing."

"I don't get that," Shanna says. "Cooking is a drag. I have to cook three nights a week, and I hate it every time. I would rather trade with Brendan and do the cleanup instead."

"Maybe you should try making something other than mac and cheese," Erykah teases.

Shanna looks offended. "I do! Haven't you heard of frozen pizza?"

Erykah snorts. "I don't mind cooking." She turns to me. "What about you? Do you like it?" Her tone is friendly.

I shrug.

She tries again. "Did you make that?" She points to my Greek salad in its glass container. I like the glass. It's a little heavy, but glass is so much nicer to eat from than plastic.

And Papa says plastic gives you cancer.

I shake my head at Erykah's question. It's a lie, but I don't want to talk with them. I don't want to make friends. I want to stay invisible. That way nobody can ever find out about my crazy dad.

"Oh," Erykah says, looking disappointed. She studies me briefly, then flashes a small smile. It's not unkind. "Well, it looks yummy too." But when I don't say anything else, she turns back to Shanna. "So what did Kennedy say when Mrs. Cristante told her about the new soccer uniforms?"

I breathe a sigh of relief.

Ice Queen 1, Friendly Girl 0.

Tomorrow I'll go back to eating beside my locker. Awesome.

Thanks a lot, Papa.

In social studies, I get mad at Papa all over again. Mr. Wilson is asking us how the Silk Road contributed to cultural exchange over the hundreds of years it was used. Nobody cares. Nobody is even awake. People are slumped in their desks, eyes glazed. One guy is trying to burn the clock to a crisp with his stare. Carey and Yannick are playing a covert game of Battleship, their grid paper hidden behind a propped-up binder.

How is it possible that nobody else finds this subject fascinating? People from all over India and Persia and China walked and rode camels and lived in caravans so they could trade with each other. We used to talk about these kinds of things at the dinner table.

Papa would tell stories about the families who lived through wars and uprisings. We'd talk about the famines and plagues throughout history. Our conversations were huge and awesome.

Until Mamma went into the hospice, and Papa stopped talking about history.

When she died a few weeks later, he stopped talking about anything. For the last year and a half, all the conversation at our dinner table has been handled by public radio.

"Even though we call it the Silk Road," Mr. Wilson is saying now, "it was actually a number of different trading routes." He points to the big map that's projected up on the screen. "Tea from China. Oil and chilies from India. Jade from Tibet. Wool rugs from Iran." He taps the side of his head. "Think about it, people. How would exchanging these things have helped the traders learn about each other's cultures?"

Mr. Wilson looks around the room. His eyes settle on me, probably because I'm the only person paying attention. I look away, but it's too late.

"Daniela?" he asks. "Any ideas?"

I open my mouth. Then I close it again.

A hot blush creeps up my face as people turn in my direction. At my old school, I would have had my hand up, ready to answer. I would have been full of ideas and questions. But that was the old me. The new me is low-key. Incognito.

And that's how it has to stay.

I shake my head. "No," I say.

"You sure? You looked like the wheels were turning."

I shake again, keeping my eyes on the floor.

Mr. Wilson turns to the class again. "Come on, eighth grade. Think! I'm a trader from India." He hikes across the room to dramatize his point. "I travel for a few days on this trading route, and when I get to the end of my section, a few guys from Pakistan are waiting there to buy my stuff. Let's say it's sandalwood, bound for Spain." He mimes handing over a package and then pocketing some money. "After that, the Pakistani traders will hop in their boats and cross the Arabian Sea, and they'll sell my stuff to the people from Iran. How does that lead to—"

"Aren't India and Pakistan enemies though?" Samir interrupts.

I take a breath, then give a little half nod. It's true they fight. But they didn't always.

The guy next to me catches me nodding. His name is Gregor. He's another friendly person. He has tried to get me to talk. He's wearing skinny jeans, Converse shoes and glasses with black frames. He dresses like a hipster, but I think he's actually a nerd. I've seen him reading a model-train catalog.

How many eighth-grade guys do that for kicks?

When our eyes meet, he raises one eyebrow.

I look away.

Delighted that someone in his class is actually alive, Mr. Wilson turns in Samir's direction. "More recently, yes, they have been at war," he says. "But during the peak years of trade along the Silk Road, that area was mostly peaceful. Both countries were simply India back then."

I want to add that the British split India apart in the late 1940s during Partition. More of Papa's stories shimmer to the surface of my mind. I would love to take part in this discussion.

But it's because of him that I can't.

Chapter Five

My eyes feel like someone blew a fistful of sand into them. Last night I woke up seventy thousand times because of the windstorm. It felt like a giant pair of hands was trying to tear the house apart. Everything was creaking and groaning and shaking. The shaking was the scariest. When the sky started getting light just after six, I gave up on trying to sleep and got up.

The wind blew another dozen shingles off the house in the night. They were scattered all across the lawn and driveway this morning. Our house is slowly falling apart.

"Papa," I say at breakfast, "the roof needs fixing."

He pours cream into his coffee and stirs. *Viva Italia!* proclaims the handle of the spoon he's using. "It can't be fixed," he booms. Even when he's only a few feet away, Papa sounds commanding and stern. *La voce di Dio,* Mamma used to tease. The voice of God.

"Why not?" I ask.

He takes a sip of his coffee, then stirs in a bit more cream. "There are already two roofs. One on top of the other." He gestures toward the ceiling. "The whole thing has to be replaced."

"Can you phone someone and have it replaced?" I know it's not a question of money. When Mamma was sick, he spent money on every possible thing that might make her better. After the chemo and the radiation, they tried reiki. Acupuncture. Naturopathic medicine. Garlic, fish oil and ginseng tea by the tubful. Traditional Chinese medicine. Ayurvedic medicine.

Mamma went along with all of it until it became too much. When the doctors finally suggested taking out pretty much everything inside and "washing her out" with chemicals, she told Papa she was done.

She lived three weeks after that.

These days the only thing Papa spends money on is paint for his signs.

"I will phone the roofers," Papa says as he drifts down the hall toward his room.

But he won't. He always tells me he'll take care of things, and then he never does. It's gotten to the point where I do everything, because I know he won't get around to it. Last spring I climbed up on the roof and cleaned out the gutters when waterfalls sprouted from our eaves one day during a heavy rain. I collected enough leaves that day to fill four orange garbage bags.

When Mamma was sick, I did everything because Papa was busy researching a cure. And now that she's gone, I still do everything.

I clear the table and scrape the remaining oatmeal into a bowl. I'll make spice muffins with it later. *Never waste a thing*, Mamma said. *There is always something lovely you can make from even the littlest leftovers.*

Her face smiles at me as I rinse the dishes and put them into the dishwasher.

"Why did you have to leave?" I hiss. "He's useless without you. Now I have to look after him." Sudden tears sting my eyes. "But nobody's looking after me." My voice cracks on the last words.

Every day, I do as Mamma asked me. I try to care for Papa as well as I can. I try to forgive him and remember that he loves me even if he is too sad to show it. I try to remember that he is grieving.

But I'm grieving too.

I watch him shuffle into the front hallway and pick up his briefcase, getting ready to teach. And then after class he'll go find someplace to stand with his signs. Hours and hours of warning people away from the poison he is convinced killed his wife.

What would life be like if he spent that time fixing the house?

What if he spent it with me?

By the time afternoon classes start, I am ready to lie right down on the floor and take a nap. But I don't. Instead, I put my head down on my desk and close my eyes to rest for a second.

A thump below me jerks me awake.

I blink as the classroom takes shape around me again. Math. I lift my head and wipe my mouth in a single movement. One can never be too careful about the drool factor.

The fluorescent lights are too bright against the blue carpet. Ms. Kapoor is making her way along the rows, checking people's work.

Behind me, that Gregor guy smiles. "You were sleeping," he whispers. He must have kicked my desk to wake me up.

"Thanks," I say, making a face to show him how embarrassing it is to fall asleep in class.

He laughs quietly. He has nice blue eyes. Today he's wearing a gray slouchy knit cap and red glasses. His T-shirt says *Never trust an atom. They make up everything.*

I am tempted to smile back. Instead, I turn around. No making friends with the natives.

I have time to scratch out three more answers on my page before Ms. Kapoor makes it to my spot.

When Gregor thumps my desk again, I ignore it. I'm feeling grumpy now. It's partly because I'm always grumpy when I wake up and partly because I just remembered I have to clean up those stupid shingles when I get home. And call the roofers.

I glance at the clock. Papa is probably in his Volvo now, driving to his afternoon preach-a-thon. Or maybe he's walking. He often does if he's preaching in the neighborhood. I wonder where he'll be today. Will he be informing the nice people that *FROZEN PIZZA = DEATH BY SODIUM, FAT AND CHEMICALS*, or will he simply be pointing out that *BACON KILLS*? I guess he could do both. He's got a few signs to work with.

At least he gave up trying to hand out flyers. People just scurried in the opposite direction when they saw him coming.

I try to think about something that makes me happy.

Cooking always does the trick. Maybe tonight can be peanut-chicken skewers with a Thai noodle salad. Except I won't put any sugar into the dressing this time—Papa was able to taste it last time. I think it'll still work okay without sugar. A little extra ginger maybe. Or honey. Yes, honey. From what I've read, it's got lots of healthy qualities, even though it has some natural sugars in it.

White sugar has been banned from our kitchen. Brown sugar was quick to follow. And forget the sugar replacements. *All chemicals*, Papa stormed. *And anyway, you know how sugar is produced?*

White death, he calls it.

So no sugar.

But as far as I know, he hasn't vetoed bee barf.

Chapter Six

Mrs. Wong pulls into her driveway as I'm picking up the last of the shingles. After I got out onto the lawn I discovered a hundred more little bits of asphalt. The shingles are so old that they're coming off in pieces.

I don't expect Mrs. Wong to say anything to me. They've always been friendly neighbors. They used to come to our gigantic Labor Day barbecue every summer, but things have cooled in recent months. It's not just the Wongs. A lot of people who used to come by while Mamma was sick stopped soon after she died. Not because they didn't care about me and Papa. But they got tired of hearing Papa talk endlessly about bad food. It's hard to stop him once he gets going.

Not many people come by our house anymore.

Mrs. Wong's car door closes. She sees me looking and gives a little wave as she goes inside the house. I wave back, holding my bucket of busted asphalt under one arm. I notice then that a bunch of shingles have blown onto their lawn too. I start picking them up.

By the time I've finished dumping the broken shingles into our garbage bin, the crows are doing their twilight flyover. They do it every day, flocking

44

by the hundreds over our neighborhood on their way to the protected bay at the north end of the city. I watch the black stream in the sky, wishing that my life could be like theirs—simple, straight-forward, driven only by the search for food. No grief. No embarrassment. No need to hide.

One final crow straggles way behind the others. I decide it's a girl. Her wings beat steadily, but the distance between her and the rest of the flock doesn't get any smaller. She does not call out. She does not pump harder. She simply keeps going, not looking around, not looking down. I wonder what her story is. Does she not want to be with the rest of the mob? Is there something she's avoiding? Something she is dreading?

Or maybe that's not it at all.

Maybe she just doesn't know if she belongs anymore.

Chapter Seven

I am thinking about the crows when
I board the bus after school the next
afternoon. There's a real bite to the
November air. The rains will be settling
in soon. Suits me. Rain means it's
time for soups and stews. Tonight is
potato–leek chowder with smoked
salmon, cream and parmesan. The
salmon substitutes nicely for bacon.

Papa doesn't fuss much about salmon. He will rant about mercury in tuna, but I suspect he likes salmon too much to find fault with it.

I take a seat and unwind my scarf from around my neck. I'm just opening my book when I feel someone else sit down beside me. I move over without looking up.

"Wow, what's that about?" asks a familiar voice.

I look up. My tummy does a little flip. Uh-oh.

Gregor is staring down at the book in my lap. *Intercourses*, the cover says. Behind the title is a picture of a nearly naked woman sitting in a pile of luscious red strawberries.

I blush. "It's a cookbook." Quickly I open it up. I hope he doesn't make any wisecracks about the title.

"Wow. What kind of cooking?" he asks, staring down at the pages.

Oh cripes. Of all the pages it could have opened to, it had to be the one with the half-naked guy smeared all over with chocolate sauce.

"Uh," I say, "all kinds. Food mostly."

I wish I could drop through the floor. This is so awkward. I don't want him to be sitting next to me. Well, I do, but I don't.

I pretend to read. When I turn the page—being careful to skip over the picture of the woman in the asparagus skirt—he speaks again.

"What do you like to cook?" he asks.

I ignore him. No friends. No complications.

Still, ignoring him feels awful. It's so *rude* to ignore people. I imagine what Mamma would say. She would not approve of me treating anyone this way.

Gregor doesn't give up easily. Either he's really nice, or he's really persistent, or he's really dumb. What-ever he is, he says, "I bet you like to make cupcakes."

I lift my head and glare at him. "Are you saying I'm fat?"

His eyes widen. "No," he says, shaking his head. "I—no. No, not at all." He blinks, clearly flustered. I can tell he wasn't saying that.

I turn back to my cookbook. I'm not offended. I do have a big bum, but it doesn't bother me. Actually, I kind of like it. The only person who has ever teased me about it was a scarecrow-skinny girl at Spruce Cliff, and I'd rather have curves than spikes, thanks.

But it was a good opportunity to shut him down. Maybe *now* he won't bug me. I flip the page huffily for good measure.

"I just thought that girls like cupcakes," he says. "I see now that it was an ill-conceived generalization."

He talks nerdy. It's sort of cute. But that doesn't matter, because I'm not going to let him in.

"I'm not most girls," I sniff.

"You certainly are not."

I look at him through narrowed eyes.

He lifts his hands in surrender. "I mean that in a good way," he says. "You're not the same as other girls. You're different."

"Different how?" I snap. I'm kind of good at being mean.

"I don't know. You don't travel in a pack with other girls. You think about stuff. And"—he points to the book—"you read cookbooks for fun."

I feel a blush creeping up my neck, and I rearrange my scarf. We're fifteen minutes from my house. I am praying we get to his stop quickly so he can get off and go home.

Come to think of it, I have never seen him on this bus before.

"So then," he says, "if you don't like making cupcakes, what *do* you like to make?"

I sigh theatrically.

He waits.

I roll my eyes. "Pasta," I say shortly.

"Really? Are you Italian?"

I nod, once.

"What's your last name?"

"Müller."

"Myooler?" He repeats it slowly. "That doesn't sound very Italian."

"It's German. My dad's last name," I say.

"Is he very German?"

"What do you mean, *is he very German*?"

"Like, was he born in Germany?"

"Oh. Yeah. He grew up near the Black Forest, but he moved here to go to university. My mother's last name was Rizzuto." You would think an Italian and a German would make an odd pairing, but it's kind of perfect. They are both loud talkers with heavy accents who love to argue and interrupt each other.

At least, they used to.

Gregor's eyes light up. "Really? Rizzuto? That's a last name too?"

"Um, yeah. What do you mean, *too*?" This guy is confusing to talk to.

"I love rizzuto!" he exclaims. "It's really good. My grandmother always makes it for Thanksgiving. Hers has a lot of parmesan in it. And wild mushrooms."

"That's *risotto*," I say. Oh my god. I have to bite the insides of my lips to keep from laughing. He's hopeless.

"Oh." He looks puzzled for a moment and then a flash of embarrassment crosses his face. When he smiles again, my whole energy field lights up.

I look back at my book.

"Risotto," he repeats. "I have been saying it wrong for a very long time."

I pretend to read.

"So you like pasta," he says after a moment. "I like lasagna. What's your favorite kind?"

He is *not* going to leave me alone. "Spaghetti carbonara," I say briskly. I don't take my eyes off the page.

"What's in that?"

Why didn't I just pick mac and cheese?

I sigh. "Cream. Garlic. Cheese. Pepper. Egg. Pancetta. Except I leave that out."

"What is pancetta, and why do you leave that out?"

"It's an Italian-style bacon."

"And why do you leave it out?" he repeats.

I sigh and look up. "Haven't you heard? Bacon isn't very good for you."

Gregor covers his ears, a look of mock horror on his face. "Speak no evil about bacon! I won't hear it."

I fight a smile, which probably makes me look like I just swallowed vinegar.

Gregor uncovers his ears and grins. "Did you know they had a bacon festival last year downtown?"

I give up trying to be cold to him. I want to know more about this bacon festival. We end up talking about all the things that can be made with bacon. We decide there should be a national bacon museum. With a store that sells bacon, of course, and little things made from bacon.

"Like pen holders and clocks," Gregor says. "And knit caps."

My stomach hurts from laughing so much. We're about five minutes away from my house now. "So where's your stop anyway?" I ask once I've got a handle on my giggling.

Gregor shrugs. "I don't live anywhere near here."

"Then how come you're on this bus?"

He shrugs again. "Because you are."

My face goes all hot again. He caught my bus because he wanted to hang out with me? What about his nerdbot friends? Every time I pass him in the hallway, he's talking a mile a minute to someone. This morning it was Mr. Adams, our principal. He was nodding as Gregor talked, and as they turned into the Foods room, Gregor's hands started flapping around, and Mr. Adams laughed.

Mr. Adams doesn't laugh often.

Gregor is a shapeshifter like that though. People of all stripes seem to like him.

I look out the window. We're just passing Spruce Cliff Village. I don't see Papa outside the Origins. That means he could be loose in the neighborhood. I wish Gregor hadn't taken this bus. What if he sees Papa?

Gregor is talking about bacon again, but my mind is skipping around in a near panic. I can't risk Gregor finding out about Papa. I let the bus go three stops past my usual one before I pull the cord.

"This is me," I say, standing. "I'll see you at school tomorrow."

He looks confused by my rapid conversational dismount. "Oh. Okay. See you tomorrow then."

"Yeah." I give him a quick smile, then hurry off the bus.

The cold wind sweeps through my tights when I hit the sidewalk. It makes me shiver. I walk in the opposite direction of home in case Gregor is watching from the window.

I scold myself all the way home. What am I thinking, making friends with someone from school? If Gregor finds out my dad is the Food Freak—and if other people catch on—my life at Central is over.

Chapter Eight

Of course Mr. Wilson assigns us a major project later that week. And of course we have to work with a group.

"Can't we work alone?" Kennedy asks.

Mr. Wilson shakes his head. "All through life you're going to have to work with other people," he says. "Besides, research shows that when you work with others, you develop more ideas."

Kennedy groans. I do too, inside. The last thing I want is to work with a bunch of other people. Then I'll have to actually *talk* to them.

"Well then, can't we just work with one other person?" Kennedy whines.

Mr. Wilson considers this. "Yes," he says finally. "I would prefer a group of at least three, but if you insist on working with only a partner, I won't stop you."

So, of course, because fate is not on my side, Gregor asks me to be his partner. I guess it's better him than anyone else. I don't want to have to get to know any more people than necessary.

"Sure," I say.

"So," he says after everyone has broken out into their groups. "Imperial China? The Renaissance? Or the Reformation?"

I shrug. "Each of them is going to be interesting to learn about. Do you have a preference?"

"Are you serious? It all sounds ultra boring to me," he says. He pushes his glasses higher on his nose and studies the handout. "Hmm. There's nothing here about how bacon shaped civilization. Now *that* I could get into."

I snort. A couple of people across the room look in our direction. I make my face blank. "Why don't you like history?" I ask when everybody has gone back to their own conversations.

Gregor sighs and looks at the ceiling. "It all happened a long time ago. And all of the people involved are dead now anyways. How is any of that important to my life?"

This is what Papa says about why people don't like history. "But our world now was totally shaped by everything people did before," I say to Gregor. I love learning how people used to live. "*Totally*. Without Apple, we wouldn't have the iPad, right? But if the Industrial Revolution hadn't happened, we never would have invented computers two hundred years later. If the Middle East hadn't always been a zone of unrest, Steve Jobs's dad would never have immigrated to the United States."

Gregor looks at me. "You really like this stuff."

I shrug. "My dad's a history professor." It slips out before I can think about it. Arrgh. Okay, that's *all* I'm going to say about him.

"Must be nice," he says. "My dad's a loser." There's a bitter edge to his voice.

"Oh," I say. "Does that pay well?"

He shoots me a look that's halfway between irritation and laughter.

"Sorry," I say. "My dad's not perfect either."

"Yeah," he says. "Parents suck most of the time."

I think of Mamma. And I think of Papa before she died. They didn't suck.

"What's wrong with your dad?" I ask.

He shrugs. It's the first time I've seen him anything close to angry. "Oh, you know. He cracked up and started doing weird stuff in the operating room."

"He's a surgeon?"

"Was."

"He's not anymore?"

"He's not allowed to practice right now."

"How come?" As soon as I say the question out loud, I wish I hadn't. It's too nosy.

Gregor shrugs. "Oh, nothing major or anything. Just showing up for surgery drunk as a skunk. Swearing and yelling when he doesn't get his way. Refusing to take off his sunglasses."

"During a surgery?"

"Yeah. They're talking about taking his license away."

I sit there staring at Gregor. He has just blown this big, fragile bubble of truth in my direction, and I am terrified of catching it the wrong way and making it pop.

"Wow, that's a lot," I finally say.

He nods again. "Yeah, there's more. He ditched me and my mom and my brother. Just took off."

"Wow." I drop my voice to a whisper. "Do you still see him?"

"Nope. And he won't tell my mom where he is."

"Is she okay?"

He shrugs again. It's bitter this time. "She'll never be okay. She's mortified. People feel sorry for her. It drives her crazy."

"That must be really frustrating."

He nods, then shakes his head quickly, like he's clearing it. "Anyway. Whatever. It could always be worse. We're healthy, and we have a roof over our heads. At least, that's what my mom always says." He grins. "And I get to partner on this project with someone who reads cookbooks for fun. *Dirty* cookbooks," he adds in a stage whisper, peeking around.

It cracks me up, but I am careful not to laugh out loud. "It wasn't dirty!" I exclaim. "I got it from the library."

"Yeah, from the *dirty* section," he whispers.

I laugh.

"What about you?" he asks.

"What about me?"

"What about your family?"

I wish I hadn't asked about his dad. Because what did I think, that he wouldn't ask me about mine?

"It's boring," I say, with what I hope is an easy wave. "You know. The usual family stuff. Let's get going on this so we don't have too much to do outside class." I slide the assignment sheet out from under his pen and read from it. "So here it looks like we need to describe gender roles, daily life and family structures."

Gregor leans forward on his elbows, so he's less than a foot from my face. "Nothing bores me. I could sit in a padded cell for eighteen years and never run out of things to think about."

Why am I not surprised? This guy could probably rewrite the entire *Hunger Games* trilogy in binary code.

"But history bores you," I say, indicating the assignment sheet.

He pauses, then grins. "Touché."

"Indeed." I make a show of rummaging in my bag for my favorite black pen.

"But I still want to know about your boring family."

"Nothing to report," I say.

"Oh, come on," he says. "I told you about mine."

This is true. He told me a whole lot about his family. He opened up and took a chance. In a normal friendship, this is where you reciprocate. Share something of similar value. But I just can't.

Besides, I never asked him to tell me all that personal information about his dad. He went ahead and did it. I don't want to be responsible for that.

He's waiting for me to say something. I'm feeling a little desperate. I flip the paper over to the blank side and start making notes. "I think we should do the Renaissance. The Reformation is heavy on religion. The Renaissance is more interesting. And besides," I say, looking up with a smile I hope he thinks is easy-going, "it started in Italy."

"Ah, Italy," Gregor says. He leans back in his chair and kisses his fingers in a Mafioso-like way. It's kind of funny, because he is so not a godfather type. "Were you born there?"

"Nope," I say. "Just my mom. Okay, let's focus. We can get our outline done in class today if we get going."

"Okay, okay," Gregor says. "I will-a work as you say, Dani-bella." He's talking now in an exaggerated Italian accent. "But your mamma. Tell-a me about your mamma. Is-a she-a beautiful like-a you?"

His compliment confuses my response. I want to shut this conversation down, but hearing him say I'm beautiful is like tasting a chocolate truffle for the first time.

"Thanks," I manage. Then I take a deep breath and fix him with a look that says I refuse to be distracted. "Okay. So what aspects of daily life should we look at?" I sit with my pen poised over the paper.

"Why-a you-a so secretive, Dani-beautiful?" he says. He leans back in his chair and studies me in a lazy way, eyes half closed. "You-a gotta something to hide?"

I cap my pen and slap it down on the desk. "My mother is dead," I say tightly. "And my father is locked in a permanent state of grief. And I don't want to talk about it. Happy now?"

Gregor freezes, his hand halfway through stroking an invisible mustache. "Oh," he says, sitting forward in his chair. "I am really sorry. I had no idea."

"Well, now you do." I pack up my books, even though class won't be over for another half hour. I hike my bag onto my shoulder and tell Mr. Wilson I need to go to the infirmary.

I snatch the assignment sheet from Gregor's desk as I leave.

Chapter Nine

Gregor catches up with me on the bus. "Hey." He sits down beside me.

Half of me wants to scream, and the other half doesn't know what to do. I am surprised to feel a sort of excitement. I know he got onto my bus just to talk to me. But I can't be excited. I want to stay mad.

I turn to look out the window as I try to figure out which feelings I should show him.

"I'm really, super sorry," he says.

"It's okay," I say without looking at him.

"No, it's not. You tried to tell me to back off, and I didn't listen."

The sincerity in his voice melts the frost off my indignation. I flash a look at him. "It's okay."

"You sure?"

I nod. I could make it harder, but he is so earnest. And he didn't mean to hurt me. Why should I hurt him? "I was a little rude too," I admit.

He waves it off. "I deserved it. You should have punched me in the nose."

I smile at the image.

"Or maybe dished me a roundhouse kick." He does an awkward seated demonstration. I laugh.

He nods at the book I'm holding. "What do you have there? Another steamy cookbook?"

I roll my eyes. "Would you stop?" Although I'm really glad he isn't asking about my mother. That's usually the way the conversation slides once people find out she's dead.

He grins as the bus pulls away from the curb.

"It's *Watership Down*," I say. "Nothing remotely steamy."

He looks disappointed. "Oh. Well, that's too bad. No nudity?"

"They're all nude."

"Really?" He looks at the book again.

I shrug. "They're rabbits."

"Oh. Ew," he says as the inevitable thought occurs to him.

I laugh.

"Oh, hey," he says, reaching into his bag. "You left your pen on my desk."

He hands it to me in a weird way. Is he holding it like that so I can't avoid touching his fingers when I take it?

"Thanks." An electrical impulse jumps between our fingers, and I jerk my hand back. I hurry to think of something else to say. "I guess we should figure out when to work on our project…Did Mr. Wilson say anything about whether we have more class time for it?"

"I wouldn't count on it," Gregor says. "We'll definitely need to work on it outside class."

I nod. "Okay." Oh jeez. More time with him. This doesn't work with my plan.

"Saturday?" he says.

"Sure. Okay, yeah."

His eyes light up. "Awesome. How about your place?"

My palms start to sweat. "Uh, no, my place is no good." What do I tell him? My brain zings along like a car radio scanning for a station. Looking for a reasonable excuse. "My dad's really grumpy and mean," I finally stammer. "It's better not to get in his way. What about your place?"

"I don't care if your dad is grumpy."

"Well, but he's really, *really* grumpy. He doesn't like other people. At all."

Gregor smiles. "I'll soften him up. How can he not like me?" He does a Mafia godfather thing again, spreading his arms confidently, like he's the king of the world. "I'm a nice guy."

"He won't like you," I lie. "I swear. It's not even worth trying. What about your place?" I ask again.

Gregor lowers his arms, and his face closes up. "Nah," he says. "Charlie will bug us the whole timc."

"Charlie? Is that your dog?"

He laughs. "No, Charlie is my little brother."

"Oh. How old is he?"

"He's nine. And he's a brat."

"Maybe he can help us with our project."

"No," Gregor says flatly. "Let's go somewhere else."

"Okay." I'm a little disappointed. I would have liked to see where Gregor lives. I'd say Fernwood, the hippie-dippie neighborhood with flowered telephone poles and community gardens. It's funky and welcoming. I wonder what his house looks like. I bet there's a wicker chair in the living room and soft blankets thrown on the sofa. I'd like to see his room. Look at his bookshelves. See what old stuffed animals he still keeps. Maybe he has a train set.

"Where else can we go?" he asks. "Hey, I know. What about the rec center?"

"Yeah, we could go there. Or the library."

"The library," he says. "That's perfect."

"Okay," I say. I pull out my social-studies folder. "We've got a few minutes right now. Maybe we can finish that outline."

"Are you always this much of a nerd?" he says.

"Speak for yourself!" I give him a little shove.

He laughs, then shoves me right back. "I always speak for myself. Too many people say what they think other people want to hear."

"Hmm, the world needs more of you," I say, then feel embarrassed.

"Correction," he says. "The world needs more of *us*."

I open my mouth to reply, but it can't do anything except smile.

We work, then talk, then work again. We discuss PlayStation verses Xbox and why people never look at each other on buses or in elevators. Whether dogs are awesome or disgusting. Why you always wake up before you die in a dream.

I get a little twitchy when the bus nears an intersection where Papa sometimes trolls.

I look out the window.

Of course he had to be there today.

Papa is standing on the wide concrete corner beside the light standard, wearing a sign I haven't seen before. At the top is a drawing of an open hand, then the words *GIVE PALM OIL THE FINGER!* Down at the bottom of the sign is a picture of a raised middle finger. When Papa turns, I see the back of the sign. *RAINFOREST DESTRUCTION FOR YOUR MARGARINE AND LIPSTICK. AND HOW ABOUT HEART DISEASE WHILE WE'RE AT IT?*

Wow. He's broadening out now. He's not just talking about food anymore. Now he's tackling the environment.

Fantastic. That topic is endless. I might as well forget about him ever putting down his signs.

At the bus stop about twenty-five yards away, a couple of kids are goofing around and making fun of him. One of them pretends to hold up a sign. He turns this way and that, wagging his finger at the passing cars as though lecturing them. His friend gives him the finger, and they dissolve into laughter. It makes my blood boil. What do they know? If they had any idea why Papa has gone so crazy, maybe they wouldn't make fun.

This thought is followed by my own shame and embarrassment. If Papa didn't act so crazy, nobody *would* make fun.

"I've seen that guy around," Gregor says, following my gaze.

"Oh?" I say, and then my throat closes up. I fake a yawn, pretending I hardly even noticed him. *Please, please, please don't say anything mean about the weird guy standing on the street corner.*

"Yeah," Gregor says. He takes a breath, but before he can say anything else I ask him about his favorite kind of pizza. His eyes light up, and the conversation pivots. I breathe the deepest possible sigh of relief. Crisis averted.

The bus rumbles on. I participate in the conversation, but my mind is consumed with going over and over the scene at the corner. Seeing people laugh at my father makes me ache.

Eventually I realize that I have to get off at the same stop as the last time Gregor was on my bus. I let the bus roar past my usual stop as we talk about pizza toppings. After two more stops, I pull the cord. "Well, this is me," I say, pulling on my cap and tucking my frizzies in.

Gregor stands, scrambling his books and papers into his backpack. "I'll walk you home."

Hot panic seizes me. "No!" I bleat.

He looks up. I can see the question in his eyes before he even opens his mouth.

"No!" I say again. "No, I have to, uh, I have to clean up all the shingles that blew off my house in the windstorm. They're *everywhere*." I fling my arms wide to show him just how far they went.

He shrugs. "That's okay. I can help."

"No!" I say. The bus slows, and my panic careens from orange zone into red zone. "My dad's really grumpy! I told you, remember? If you come over and if he comes home from work, he'll be really mad." I'm babbling now, but I've got to stop Gregor from seeing where I live.

And seeing Papa.

His brows furrow a little. "Okay," he says, confused. "No worries. Well, I guess I'll see you tomorrow then?"

Relief rushes into my veins and crashes around inside my body. "Yes!" I sing. I can feel that my eyes are too wide, my grin is too big and my head is nodding too fast. "Tomorrow! I can't wait! Bye!"

The bus comes to a full stop. As the doors open, I leap out onto the sidewalk. I turn to wave as the bus lumbers away. A big ad is plastered across the windows, so I can't tell if Gregor is waving back. I grin and wave like crazy, then turn toward home, my heart slamming like a washing machine with an unbalanced load.

That was way too close.

Chapter Ten

I'm wrestling my curls into a fresh pony-tail when there's a knock on the door.

I look through the peephole and see that it's Gregor. I panic again. I crack the door open several inches. "What are you doing here?"

"Your doorbell doesn't work," he says.

Of course it doesn't. The doorbell hasn't worked in a year.

"Why are you here?" I demand.

He holds out *Watership Down*. "You left this on the bus. This is a common habit for you, I see. Leaving things behind." He grins.

"You followed me?"

He shrugs. "It wasn't all that hard. I got off at the next stop, then backtracked. Although I *am* trying to figure out why you walked in the opposite direction yesterday."

Oh. Of course. In my panic earlier, I got off the bus and headed directly home. I should have gone the opposite way, like I did yesterday.

I snatch the book from his hands. "You could have just brought it to school tomorrow." I open the door wider and peer beyond the porch, looking down the street in both directions. I know I'm being paranoid. Papa rarely comes home before five. He likes to catch the dinnertime shoppers.

"I wanted to see where you live," Gregor is saying.

"Well, now you've seen it," I say. I step back inside the doorway but don't invite him to come in.

Gregor pauses uncertainly. "Okay," he says. "Do you want some help picking up those shingles?" He looks at the lawn, where there are exactly zero shingles.

"No. I don't."

"Okay," he says again. He looks back at me. "Why do you get off the bus so far away? That stop is much closer to your house." He points over his shoulder with his thumb.

I steal another glance around. A tall dark figure turns the corner onto our street. His long strides carry him quickly in the direction of our house.

What? Oh no. This cannot happen.

I look at Gregor. "Why do you have to ask so many questions?" I hiss. "I have to go. I have a lot to do."

Gregor blinks, looking totally confused. I should feel awful for being so mean, but I'm much more frightened by the train wreck that's fast approaching. I have to get Gregor out of here.

"Just GO!" I shout, and he jumps.

"Okay, *okay*." He turns, but by then it's too late.

Helpless to stop anything, I watch the whole terrible scene unfold before me, like a slow-motion car accident. Gregor descends the steps and walks down the walkway slowly, his head down. I want to go inside and hide my eyes or maybe gouge them out. But I stay rooted to the spot as my nightmare takes shape.

At end of our driveway, Gregor turns toward the bus stop. He goes about twenty paces before he looks up and sees Papa coming in his direction. Papa is oblivious to Gregor. He sails past, his sandwich board flapping as he walks. He carries his tall sign by his side.

Gregor's gaze follows Papa as he passes. I close my eyes. When I open them, Gregor is still standing in the same place. He watches Papa turn the corner at our hedge and start up our driveway.

I go inside and close the door before Gregor can see my face.

Chapter Eleven

At supper, my thoughts bubble. What is Gregor going to say tomorrow? Will he say anything? Or will he ignore me and pretend he never even knew me?

For sure he's never going to take my bus again.

Jordan Rigby's costume swims up in my mind. I can see Peyton laughing.

I watch Papa eat his basil-and-red onion pizza on whole-grain crust. His beard bobs as he chews, his eyes locked on a spot on the table six inches in front of him. He's probably concocting a message to paint on his next sign. A thread of cheese dangles from the side of his mustache.

I hate him.

I manage to keep my temper until we get through the salad and the pizza. But once I'm up and clearing the dishes, I can't stand it any longer.

I set the dirty plates down on the counter with a crash. "You know, maybe you should see someone."

Papa doesn't even look up from the newspaper. "Hah?" he asks absently.

"You know. Someone you can talk to. A psychologist or a grief counselor or something like that."

"I talk to someone." He licks his finger and turns the page, then continues reading.

"You do? Who?"

"I don't need to tell you that."

"It's not enough to talk to *yourself*, Papa," I say.

"Dani." His voice carries a warning.

"What?" I say. "You need help, Papa. You need someone to help you get over Mamma so that you can live a normal life again."

Papa recoils like I've thrown hot water on him. We never speak of Mamma. Never.

He stares at me for a moment. I am a little scared of myself. For myself.

"That's enough," he says. His voice is quiet.

Fury flash-heats my skin. "No, it's not *enough*!" I shout. I slap my hand on the counter. "Do you think it's normal for you to wander random street corners, waving signs that tell people they're going to die? That's not normal."

"Dani." His voice is calm, but his face is as rigid as stone. "It's not me who needs help. It's not me who is abnormal. It's all the lazy people who put their lives at risk because they want convenience." He sweeps a hand across the room, his voice rising. "It's the manufacturers who pour vast quantities of salt and preservatives into—"

"Stop it!" I scream. I slap the counter again, hard. My elbow knocks a fork handle. It flips off the plate, catapulting a gob of salad into the air. Spinach splats against the side of the fridge. The fork clangs to the floor. Pain roars through my palm, then dulls to a hot, sharp throbbing.

Papa blinks.

"You don't need to make an idiot of yourself to tell people your opinion!" I say.

"I am not making an idiot—"

"Yes, you are!" I scream. A small part of me can't believe I'm shouting these words at my own father. It feels very wrong. My father is not a man you should ever shout at.

But I'm sick to death of him. "Why can't you be normal?" I cry. "Why don't you just…write letters to the editor or something? Everyone thinks you're a weirdo. They avoid you. They stare at you. Don't you see that?" I'm being unbelievably cruel, but I need him to understand.

Papa folds his hands on the table in front of him. "Dani," he says calmly. "In this day of short attention spans, I find it necessary—"

"To *what*, Papa?" I shout. "To ruin my life?" I look around, my rage needing a physical outlet. I pick up an empty glass and throw it against the wall. It smashes into a million shards that scatter under the fridge and the table.

"Daniela." Papa stands. His voice is sharp. "That's enough."

"No, Papa, *I've* had enough. I've told you a hundred times, but you never listen." I storm into the living room and snatch up one of his large poster boards. *PROCESSED FOODS = DEVIL SPAWN = SICKNESS & DEATH,* it says. I tear it in half. "I had to change schools because everyone at Spruce Cliff was making fun of you," I say. My voice is thick with tears. "I lost all my friends." I tear the poster in half again. "First Mamma died." The words hit him like a blow. Too bad. All we do is tiptoe around the fact that she isn't with us anymore. "And now, do you know what they call you?" I rip the poster again, my eyes angry, narrow slits. "They call you the Food Freak!"

Papa stares at me, his mouth slightly open.

"You're wrecking my life, Papa!" I shout. "And none of it is going to bring Mamma back!" I throw the little ripped-up pieces of paper at him, but they just flutter down onto the coffee table and the piano bench.

I turn, shaking and sobbing, and stumble toward my room.

Chapter Twelve

Papa knocks, but I don't answer. When he begins talking to me through the door, I put a pillow over my head.

I wait until he goes away.

I don't go to school the next day. I go to the rec center and sit looking at the pool. Only Papa ever went into the big pool with me. We used to play on the pirate ship. Mamma always sat in the warm pool with all the babies, watching us.

It's been years since I've been swimming, I realize. I stopped when Mamma got sick.

Everything stopped when Mamma got sick.

I stay at the rec center all day. I buy my lunch in the cafeteria, then my dinner. I read all the free magazines in the racks by the stairs. I wander around in the bleachers above the pool, watching the swim teams practice. Through the windows overlooking the pool I can see people sweating as they run on the treadmills in the gym.

When the rec center closes at eleven, I think about taking the bus back home. But I don't feel like going back. I want as much distance between Papa and me as possible. And it's not like I've got anyone else I can stay with.

I root through the lost and found for a towel. At the bottom of the box I find a granola bar, its wrapper wrinkled and old. I eat it in three bites. It tastes like sawdust. I hide out in the change rooms until the lights go out. Then I creep back out onto the pool deck by the light of the emergency exits. It's depressing to be in here all alone. Maybe I should have gone home. But it's too late now—the buses stop running at midnight. I decide to sleep on the trampoline the dive team uses for training.

Except I can't really sleep. The towel is crunchy and smells stale. I haven't brushed my teeth, and the chlorine in the air hurts my eyes.

"I can't handle it anymore, Mamma," I whisper. "Papa is ruining my life. He's chased away all my friends. And I can't make any more." I blink hard as the tears come. My nose starts to run. I wipe it on the towel. Ugh. This keeps getting worse.

I wish Mamma would answer me. I wish she could be *here*. She would know what to do. She wouldn't have let things get this bad. None of this would be happening if she hadn't died.

"What should I do, Mamma?" I beg. "Where can I go?"

Silence.

Maybe I can fly to Italy and live with Auntie Carlotta. But their place is really small. And things are tight for them right now. Mamma said they don't sell as much cheese as they used to. But maybe I could help out. I wouldn't have to be a burden. I could look after my little cousins for Auntie Carlotta, and then maybe she could go find other work and Uncle Silvio could still do the cheese. I bet Mamma would be okay with that idea.

But then again, would Mamma want me to leave Papa? Especially after I promised to take care of him? And where would I live anyway? Carlotta and Silvio have only two bedrooms for the four of them. They rent out the rest of the house to travelers.

I sleep poorly. When morning comes, I am exhausted. It will be the second school day I've skipped in a row, but I don't care. I bet the school doesn't care either. It feels crazy. I just ran away from home and slept in a rec center. Whose life is this?

I splash water over my face in the change-room sink. I look like roadkill. The paper towel is rough, but it's better than using that disgusting thing I slept under. All of a sudden it hits me that I could have used Papa's VISA card to stay in a hotel.

I stop drying my face for a second to think about this.

Huh. Maybe not Italy. But I could use the card to buy myself a bus ticket to a different city. To a whole different life. I'm pretty sure he wouldn't drag his damn signs across the country to follow me.

I stand there with the paper towel crunched up around my face for several long seconds as I consider the possibility of running away for real. The fantasy devours me.

I only have a few years of school left. Maybe I could get a part-time job in a bakery, or in a restaurant kitchen as a prep cook.

I catch sight of myself in the mirror. I hold my own gaze for a moment, asking whether I've actually got the guts to do this.

But who would take care of Papa? Without me, he wouldn't eat. He would wear the same clothes day in and day out. What would happen to him? It's bad enough that he lost his wife. He would probably lose his mind if his own kid walked out on him.

I close my eyes and rub them as the familiar heaviness settles back on me. I can't leave. Papa would wither and die.

But how do I keep myself from doing the same?

Chapter Thirteen

Papa's car is still in the garage when I get home. It surprises me. I thought he'd be at work. It's Wednesday, after all. I expected to have the house—and the day—to myself. I thought I could clean up the mess I made before he noticed.

No way I can face school today. Not with Gregor there.

I go in through the laundry room, hoping Papa won't hear me. I forget about the door sensor. It pings as the door opens.

"Dani?" Papa's voice comes from the other end of the house.

Crap.

Quick footsteps approach. Papa's face appears around the corner. "Dani," he says. I hear the relief in his voice. In his hands he holds a dishtowel that's been twisted into a tight coil. "Where did you go? I was terrified." His voice cracks. He lets go of the dishtowel. It unspools sloppily as he reaches for me. "I was so frightened that you had gone." He looks so old all of a sudden.

Guilt surges inside me. I never expected him to react like this. Tears spring to my eyes.

Before I can turn away or lower my head, Papa grabs me in a fierce hug. He squashes my face to his chest, and one of the buttons on his shirt digs into my cheekbone.

But right now? I couldn't care less.

My father is holding me in his arms. *My father*.

My father is *talking* to me. Asking me where I've been.

Holding me.

"I slept at the pool," I say. My voice is muffled against his shoulder. He smells like laundry detergent and...Papa.

Him.

"You were where?" He loosens his grip so I can speak.

I straighten and he lets me go, but I can't look at his face. Not yet. "I was at the rec center," I say. "I slept on the trampoline." It feels like an absurd thing to say. Kevin appears from around the corner. He pauses to survey the scene, then glides gently across the floor toward me, his shoulder blades rolling smoothly under his fur.

"You slept on the trampoline?" Papa repeats. "At the rec center?"

I nod. "It wasn't very comfortable." The cat rises up, puts his front paws on my thighs and stretches.

"Why, Dani?"

I shrug. I gently pick Kevin's claws out of my jeans. He drops to the floor and stalks back in the direction he came from.

Papa hugs me again. "Because of me," he whispers. "Because I've been lost in my own world. I've forgotten about you."

I start to cry then, small stinging tears, as though I am afraid of anything bigger. In case they swallow me and Papa whole. "I'm sorry I worried you," I snuffle. I pull away from his hug. "And I'm sorry I shouted at you. And threw the glass. And tore up your poster."

Papa is quiet for a moment. "I think I understand." Then he shakes his head. "I didn't know you changed schools because of me."

"Did you know I changed schools at all?"

He looks at me with sad eyes. "No. I did not."

I nod. Somehow this hurts more than anything else.

"I am sorry, Dani."

I shrug.

"Was it really that bad?"

I think about the way people looked at me. The mean pity in their eyes. *You know Dani? Poor girl. Her mom died of bowel cancer, and then do you know what happened? Her dad went frickin' crazy.*

When I try to answer, my throat closes. I shrug again.

"I embarrass you," Papa says now.

I can hear the hurt in his voice. The worry. I want to save him from it. I don't want to hurt Papa. But it's the truth. He embarrasses me to death.

"Yes, Papa," I whisper.

He sags back against the dryer.

"I know you have an important message," I say. "And I actually agree with it." I look up into his face. "I'm with you on the sugars and fats and chemicals. These things *do* make us sick. They might even have made Mamma sick."

"They *did* make Mamma sick." Right away there's a furious edge to his voice.

I nod. I will never argue this with Papa. He will never change his opinion, even though the doctors couldn't say what caused Mamma's cancer.

"But the way you're telling people makes you look crazy," I continue. "People end up avoiding you."

"And making fun of me."

It is such a relief to be having this conversation. I don't know what I expected it would be like when we finally did talk about this stuff—if we ever did. But Papa hasn't lost touch as much as I had feared. He's actually hearing me.

"Yes." I pick up the dishtowel from where he dropped it and start to fold it. "And when people see you as something to make fun of, your message doesn't get through."

"Then how do I make them see?" He sounds genuinely puzzled. "If I don't tell them, how do I make them see?"

I look at him. Really? He really doesn't have a clue? He thought that wearing signboards and holding placards that talk about Satan and destiny would make people listen seriously to what he has to say?

"I don't know for sure," I admit. "Letters to the editor, maybe. I mean, people do still read the newspaper. Or a YouTube documentary. Even a class at the university. Like a night class for adults. *How to shop and eat local, healthy foods*. Or a Vine," I say. "Although you'd have to set up a Facebook or Twitter page for that."

"A vine?" His face is puzzled.

His confusion makes me smile a little. "A Vine is a super-short video. You could make it funny. That always gets people's interest. Ms. Kirstein is always saying a message has more power if it stirs people's emotions. If it makes them mad, or if it makes them laugh."

He looks at me like he's seeing me for the first time. "These are good ideas. Why didn't I ask you before?"

"I don't know. Because you were too sad. And because I was too angry."

Papa closes his eyes and rubs them with his fingers. When he takes them away, his eyes are red. "I was too sad, yes," he whispers. "I'm still so sad." He looks at me. "But I don't want to make you angry with me."

I feel my eyes filling up all over again. "Well then, would you consider not wearing the signs?" I give him a lopsided smile.

Papa rubs his eyes again and nods. "Yes. I would consider not wearing the signs." He sighs deeply, then looks at me. "Would you consider helping me make a—how do you call, a *vine*?"

"Yes." My smile is full and happy now. "Yes, Papa, I can help you make a Vine."

Chapter Fourteen

Papa gives me a ride to school just before afternoon dismissal. I feel better than I have in a long time. We talked some more this morning. We figured a few things out. I think we're going to be okay.

I'm nervous about what I have to do now though.

I wait until all the buses are at the bus circle, and then I watch. When mostly everyone has boarded their buses, I hurry toward the one I want. My heart pounds like a trip hammer as I climb the steps. It's crowded, and I don't see him.

And then I do. I work my way between the people standing in the aisle, apologizing and excusing myself as I bump and squeeze my way along. When I'm finally standing in front of Gregor, I say hi.

He looks up from his phone. "Hey! Where have you been?"

I blink. I wasn't expecting him to be so normal toward me. "Uh," I say. "Well, I had to have a meeting with my dad."

"Was that him I saw at your house the other day?"

I wince. "The guy with the signs, yeah." I nod. "Yeah. That's my dad."

"Here, sit," Gregor says. He pushes over on the seat to make room for me.

"You mean you're still talking to me?" I say as I sit.

Gregor looks confused. "Why wouldn't I be talking to you?"

"I don't know. Because my dad's a nut?"

"What? No," he says. "Actually, I was thinking about catching the bus to your place and seeing if you were okay. But then I thought maybe you wouldn't want to see me. I thought I had made you mad."

"No, no." I shake my head. "I wasn't mad. Not at you, at least." I look down. "I was pretty rude to you. I'm sorry. I just didn't want you to see my dad."

"Why not?"

I shrug. "Because I thought that if you did, you'd think my dad was crazy, like everybody else does."

"Is he?"

"No, not really," I say. "He just looks like it. You know. The signs and all."

Gregor nods. "He's eccentric."

I smile. I like that. *Eccentric*. It sounds better than crazy. "Yeah. Anyway, I stayed home to talk to him about how he needs to stop wearing signs. It's freaking people out."

"Well, he is largely correct."

I stare at him. "What do you mean?"

"What do you mean, *what do I mean*? Do you think he's wrong?"

"No," I say, surprised. "I don't think he's wrong. I just think he's a little over the top."

"I don't know if he is," Gregor says. "I think we need a million people screaming this stuff from the rooftops."

"What do you mean?" I ask.

Gregor indicates his phone. "I've been reading up on it all day. I started with palm oil. I had no idea it was so bad." He reads to me from a screen he's bookmarked. "*Wreaks havoc on forests, causes steep decline in animal populations, encourages child labor and contributes to climate change*." He looks at me. "That's some pretty heavy stuff."

I nod. "It's heavy." I wonder if Gregor has any idea how chocolate is produced. About the kids in Africa who are kidnapped to work on cacao-bean farms. Who spray pesticides on the trees without wearing any masks. Who climb trees with huge machetes to cut down the cacao pods and then drag sacks weighing more than one hundred pounds through the forest.

Does he know how sugar is produced?

And then there's what it does to our bodies when we eat it.

"I think your dad's got a point," Gregor is saying now.

"Yeah. The problem is, he's making it in such an awkward way."

"Why is all this processed-food stuff so important to him?"

I look down at my hands. "My mom died of bowel cancer. Papa—my dad— he thinks it's because of all the bad stuff in our food. He is convinced she died from the nitrates and preservatives in processed meats."

"Oh," Gregor says. He's quiet for a moment. "What if he's right? Look at this." He goes back to his phone and scrolls through a couple screens. "Here. I looked up MSG because I've seen your dad holding a sign about it. This is an article in *Men's Health*."

"MSG is in everything," I say, peering at the screen.

Gregor nods. "I know. Well, I didn't know it before, but I do now." He reads, "*MSG, or monosodium glutamate, also goes by maltodextrin, sodium caseinate, autolyzed yeast, autolyzed vegetable protein, hydrolyzed vegetable protein, yeast extract and even citric acid.*" He looks up at me. "This is terrible."

"You know what this means, don't you?"

"What?"

"No more ginger beef," I say.

"No!"

"Or ramen noodles. Or fast food."

"NO!" Gregor cries. "It's everywhere!" He fake stabs himself through the heart.

"It's everywhere," I agree.

"It's depressing." He goes back to reading what the article says. "MSG is considered a neurotoxin." He looks up. "So it poisons brain cells."

I shrug and nod at the same time.

"*Shown to damage nerve cells by overexciting them to the point of cell death*," he reads. "MSG is also a—" He peers closer, then reads slowly, "A chemoinducer—"

"A cause," I supply.

"Right. Of obesity and type 2 diabetes," he finishes. "So it makes us fat."

I give a short laugh. "MSG's got nothing on nitrates."

"Nitrates," he repeats. "That's what's in hot dogs, right?"

"And bacon."

Gregor covers his ears in horror. "It just gets worse."

I laugh.

"No wonder your dad is so worked up about this stuff."

"He's pretty worked up."

"Does he do it every day?"

"What, the signs? Yeah. Well, he still goes to work. And then after work he goes around to different places and docs the sign thing. But I talked to him about it yesterday. Because I was so embarrassed when you saw him."

"What was so embarrassing?"

"Are you serious? People laughed me out of my last school because of my dad. They called him—" I break off, shaking my head.

"What? What did they call him?"

"Nothing. Never mind. It wasn't very nice."

"Is that why you got off at a different bus stop?" he asks. "So I wouldn't find out about him?"

I nod miserably.

"Jeez," he says. He looks out the window, then back at me. "I don't know. I think it's kind of cool. Do you think he'd let me hold a sign too?"

I stare at Gregor. "Are you serious?"

"Totally serious," he says. "You can't make me say anything bad about pizza though." Then he gets this silly grin that makes me go warm all over.

I try to picture Gregor standing on a street corner with Papa, in his skinny jeans and Converse sneakers. And a sandwich board.

It totally works.

"I don't know," I say. "I just spent the morning talking him out of his sign-waving brand of activism."

Gregor's face falls. "Oh."

"But maybe he could do one last gig," I hurry to suggest.

"Like a swan song?"

"Yeah, I guess."

"Sweet!" He grins, then has another thought. "Hey, let's get a bunch of people together to do this! We could ask the Eco Crusaders. They'd be in for sure."

"The Eco Crusaders?"

"Yeah, that's the fancy name for Central's environment club. They'd totally go for something like this. And they could help us pull other people in. Maybe we could even do a flash mob!" Gregor is about to go into orbit with this idea.

I'm not so sure Papa would be down with a flash mob. But he might think it's kind of cool to have other people waving signs with him. "Maybe you should meet my dad," I say. "You know, first things first."

Gregor looks at me again, eyes shining with his big plans. "Maybe I should."

"Maybe you could come over for dinner sometime."

"Maybe I could."

"But don't get him going on sugar," I warn. "Sugar is not up for discussion. Or you'll never hear the end of it."

"I guess bacon's off the table too?"

I laugh. "Yes. But if you like noodles and cream sauce…"

"Sign me up," says Gregor. "Get it? Sign me up?" He mimes holding up a sign.

I groan. "Oh, *so* bad."

"Just wait," he says. "I got lots more where that came from." He looks at me in that way he has, and my tummy does a triple flip.

I grin. "Sign. Me. *Up*."

ACKNOWLEDGMENTS

I had the amazing support of my plotting partner, Manuela Biron, in creating Dani's story. Sixth-grade student Molly Turner gave me excellent feedback from the middle-schooler's perspective. And I owe a debt of gratitude to fellow writer Peter Jory for reading the full draft and providing comments that ultimately made *Food Freak* a better story.

Alex Van Tol is the author of thirteen books, including the Orca Currents titles *Chick:Lister* and *Oracle*. She enjoys nearly every kind of food—including bacon—and, like Dani, takes great pleasure in preparing meals for the people she loves. Alex lives in Victoria, British Columbia, with her two young sons. Learn more at www.alexvantol.com.